ACROSS SCREAMING SEAS

Across Screaming Seas

DARK FOLKLORE

Georgina Jeffery

Coblyn Press

Contents

The Sea-Dweller

On the day I met Death, I was caught in a fishing net.

She found me struggling against the rocky reef bed in a shallow bay and retreating tide. I was bleeding out. My blood stained the water in an expanding cloud while spotted catsharks dodged around my flailing limbs.

Death wore a snorkel mask and a black wetsuit. I glimpsed only her shadow first, obscured by bubbles and sand from my thrashing. She took a look at me, raced to the surface to heave in a breath, then dove down again to meet me on the bottom. Her hand flashed with silver in the murky water – a knife.

The netting was thick where it had twisted and already cut deep bruises into my skin. I continued struggling while Death patiently sawed against the fibres. One by one they frayed. She broke away again, going back up for air.

When she came back to me I had calmed, found stillness. Her eyes met mine for the first time. She jerked backward in the water, shocked. Whatever she had expected me to be – it was not me. She blew out a slow stream of bubbles as she scrutinised me, then returned to the surface to fill her lungs again.

Her next approach was more cautious. I was still bound up in horrid cords, but now I stared and watched as she worked to free me. Her eyes slid endlessly back to mine. Hers were the colour of kelp in sunlight. I knew mine to be an inky black.

The last of the netting slipped free. Death's gaze travelled to my abdomen, where a small iron spike stuck out of my grey flesh. She reached out and I backed away. My fingers curled around the spike. Her eyes widened. Frantically she shook her head. She tried to beckon me, pointing to the surface.

Up, up! her eyes screamed, already kicking herself towards the rippling sky.

She stopped short of the surface, yanked to a

sudden halt. Some of the netting, so deceptively fine and delicate, seized around her ankle. The other end was caught on the rocks of the seabed.

Death tried to tug her leg away. Futile effort. The net was stuck fast. A desperate puff of bubbles emptied her lungs of air.

I hesitated. Death had just saved my life.

I flicked my tail and painfully propelled towards her. My hands glided over the false skin covering her legs, plucked at the threads of netting. I lowered my teeth to them and cut through while Death writhed in the current. She convulsed, involuntarily glugging water.

As I freed her leg, the rest of her body went limp. I surged upwards, linking one arm around her torso, and threw us both to the surface.

We broke above the waves in a gentle sea. Sunlight fell in streams upon Death's golden hair and glistened in the water droplets on her snorkel mask. I ripped the thing off her head and gave a mighty squeeze of her middle. A gulp of seawater cascaded from her mouth. She choked, hacking on salt and sand, until her eyes blearily drifted open. They blinked slowly as she focused on me. I kept us buoyed in the water and pulled her face against my chest to give her some warmth from my skin. She murmured something: a pretty sound.

We were not far from the shore. The tide was still receding. I swam us into the shallows until my fins grazed the rocky reef bed. A small wooden pier extended into the breaking surf, and this was where I landed Death. She grasped the platform with both hands and hauled herself out of the water. She collapsed onto her stomach, forehead kissing the wood, before turning to look at me again.

I clicked a brusque thank you to her. She cocked her head quizzically, mouth parting in a little 'o' that might have been trying to reply, or simply expressing astonishment.

I arched backwards, diving under the waves again. She waited on the pier, shivering, for some time. Watching for me, I was sure. I watched her in turn, from the safety of rocks far to the left, out of sight.

Eventually she left the wooden jetty, scrambling into the dunes that walled off my quiet cove.

Holding pressure against the spike in my stomach, I dove back into the cool, dark depths of the sea. I followed the tide to deeper waters, and wound my way back to the familiar safety of the swaying kelp forests. Somewhere I hoped, foolishly, that Death would be unable to follow.

The Land-Dweller

'*L*ike a *dolphin*, Rhys!'

Rhys' bushy eyebrows met in the middle of his forehead. 'I thought you said it was a person?'

'*Like* a person. But also like a dolphin!' My hands flapped excitedly while I spoke. 'That's what its skin reminded me of. It was so smooth, and kind of rubbery. And the fins! It had a dorsal fin on the back, and fish tail from the waist down.'

'Can't have been a fish tail,' he said, tipping his nose down at me with an infuriating quirk to his smile. 'Gotta be a mammal if it was a dolphin.'

'You know what I mean,' I said.

Rhys smirked and turned back to his graphs. 'So you saw a mermaid? Is that what you're saying, Erin?'

Yes! I wanted to scream. But I clammed up. Suddenly I heard myself, as if from the outside, spouting about mermaids from a fairy tale like a crazy lady. Rhys clearly thought I was exaggerating for comic effect.

'It was probably a porpoise,' I said lamely.

'Out here?' he exclaimed, this time with both surprise and genuine enthusiasm. 'That's so cool!'

I settled for a quiet smile. 'Yes. It was.'

'Whereabouts exactly?'

I faltered. I didn't want to tell him. 'Oh, out along the cliffs. Just east of Caswell Bay.'

'Really? With all the tourists and surfers about?' The fuzzy brow crinkled again. 'Lucky. Point out where you saw it when we take the next class out.'

'Sure. Although . . .' I winced internally. '. . . about that. I was hoping I could . . . use my holiday allowance to take some time off?'

'How much?'

'. . . All of it?'

Rhys crossed his arms. He wasn't an intimidating man – he had a surfer's athletic build and warm character, and a smile that came as easily as rain. His attempt to stare me down was practically sweet.

'What for?' he asked. 'You never take time off.'

My mind raced for a believable excuse. 'There's a ... big clean-up campaign I want to join. North coast. We're going to spend a couple of weeks picking up litter along the beaches, surveying the state of the reefs. You know, doing our bit.'

He scratched his head, clearly faced with a cause he couldn't deny. 'Man, you're quite the dedicated activist, huh?'

'You know me,' I replied cheerily. 'Just like we tell our little snorkellers. Gotta be responsible if you want to keep enjoying the ocean for the future.'

'Hmm. Three weeks off at once is a lot, though.'

'Come *on,* Rhys. We have hardly any bookings right now. Peak season doesn't start 'til the end of the month! You can manage without me until then.'

He huffed and glanced out the window of our cramped mobile cabin, which overlooked the golden sands of Caswell beach. A smattering of local families were out with picnics and surf boards, enjoying the unusually perfect June weather. On the wall to the left, our rack of snorkels and loan wetsuits was conspicuously full.

'Fine,' said Rhys. 'But you better be back when the season hits.'

'I will!' I jumped with excitement and started gathering my things.

'And Erin?'

'Yeah?'

'Maybe give me some warning, next time you're off to one of these events.' Rhys twiddled his thumbs. 'I wouldn't mind coming with, you know? It's a great cause.'

My smile turned a little glassy. 'Sure thing. Bye, Rhys. And thank you!'

I threw my gear into my beat up Corsa and left, heading west along the coast. The opposite direction to Caswell Bay.

I didn't know whether the patch of shoreline where I'd found the mermaid had a proper name. I thought of it as my own space, a secluded and wild cove that was mine to explore. Parking off-road on the cliffs, it was a fifteen-minute walk through the dunes and down to a narrow pebble beach.

The water there was nicely sheltered, enclosed by curving cliffs on the right, and a long outcrop of good climbing rocks on the left. A small wooden jetty sat in the middle of the beach, standing just proud of the breaking waves. The wood was old and rotted, but still a nice place to sit and watch the sea in all weathers.

I didn't waste any time sitting and watching this time. I dumped my bag in the dunes, changed into my wetsuit, grabbed my mask, and ran straight into the cold waters of the Bristol Channel. There was no time to waste.

Because who knows whether the mermaid would still be there. What if the creature was just visiting? Or what if the incident with the net had spooked her, and she'd swum off to different waters?

I wish I'd had my camera out that day. If only I could have captured proof – for myself, as much as anyone else. How could I be certain that what I'd seen was real? Had it really been a mermaid? What if I'd just muddled up my memory during all that fraught underwater action?

But no. The image was clear in my mind.

I recalled short-cropped hair and dark eyes with short lashes. A nearly androgynous figure, as far as a human torso can convey. Only a very subtle curve of breasts led me to ascribe any gender to it at all, and even then, I found myself wondering whether I imagined this shape simply because that's what I thought a 'mermaid' ought to look like.

And then there was that blue-grey skin, so smooth, a little shiny under the sun, and rubbery to the touch. Throwing everything familiar about her into alien territory as, tracing further down, the hips melded into smooth contours of muscle, a great curving tail that ended in a large, fanned fluke just visible in the cloudy water. The dorsal fin sat behind her hips, about where the coccyx should be.

Was she a miracle of evolution, or a fairy tale brought to life? I had to know.

For the next fourteen days, I spent every hour of daylight at the cove. I alternated between sur-veying the ocean from the dunes with a pair of binoculars and spending time in the water. It was a cold sea, and even on the warmest day I couldn't manage more than an hour of swimming against the current – especially where it became choppier beyond the rocks.

I wished I was a better free diver. Rhys could hold his breath for a solid five minutes. He made it look simple, guiding our more adventurous students around kelp forests and rocky reefs with practiced ease. I could manage enough to dive down to the seabed, but a mere thirty seconds later I needed to rush back for air.

Each day, I trained my lungs to hold for just a few seconds longer. The descent became easier, and on a fine day the ocean felt serene below the waves. I attempted to search for my mermaid in a systematic pattern, picking a new square beyond the cove to explore each session. I stayed on the dunes until late into the night, lighting a small campfire for warmth – and hoping the mermaid might see it from wherever she dwelt in the ocean.

I definitely thought of her as 'my mermaid'. I had found her, and I felt a sort of entitlement to meet again. How dare the universe dangle such a thrilling mystery in front of me!

Part of me tried to kid myself, stay detached. I was there in a spirit of scientific enquiry. It was a startling discovery, an entirely unknown sea creature! I couldn't make up my mind whether to consider her an animal or a person. Her human-like features had me in knots with theories. Was she a mammal, like a dolphin, who gave milk to her young? A humanoid descended from cetaceans instead of primates?

After two futile, fruitless weeks of searching, it finally dawned on me that there was probably nothing I could do to find my mermaid if she didn't want to be found. I'd seen how she moved in the water – effortlessly, a thing born for it. She'd be able to skim away before my lumbering form even got close.

So, if I wanted to see her again, perhaps I had to persuade her to come to me.

One half of the cove was lined with narrow beach and sheer cliffs. The other side was less uniform, with a jutting bed of rocks that made for excellent climbing in low tide. In high tide, they extended far out into the waves like a natural promenade. If the sea was calm, as it usually was in this sheltered bay, then you could walk along the top of them with little worry for the waves gently lapping below your feet.

The farthest end of the rock walk was capped with a large, flattish stone. Perfect for what I had in mind.

I started with a necklace. Don't ask me why.

Something shiny seemed appropriate. It had a simple glass pendant that sparkled on the end of a silver chain in the midday sun. I watched it glimmer on the flat rock until the sea level climbed and slurped at its edges. A seagull pecked at it briefly, but by the time the tide was drawing back towards the horizon, the necklace remained otherwise untouched.

Full of impatience, I crept back out along the rocks and deposited an extra gift: a wrapped bar of chocolate from my surveillance snack supply. I pulled off the outer paper to expose the shiny foil beneath.

'I don't want to hurt you,' I called out to the retreating waves, and immediately felt silly for it.

I picked up my gear and left.

In the morning, I inspected the rocks again. The necklace had barely moved. For a split-second of elation I thought the mermaid had accepted the chocolate – until I discovered a seagull pecking at its remains on the beach. I chased after it, picking up flecks of foil in its wake. Lesson learned.

I dropped my next offering beside the necklace: an open compact mirror. I congratulated myself for that one. The mermaid had probably never seen her own reflection before. Surely it would make an irresistible prize.

This was how I continued for the rest of the week. Adding, at every low tide, a new shiny object to the pile which I was so unjustifiably certain was the key to attracting the mermaid's attention. I found myself contemplating fishermen and the pretty lures they use on the end of a fishing line – all shimmering rainbow colours, catching the light under the water.

This sparked an obvious revelation: if I wanted the mermaid to see my gifts, I ought to post them through her front door rather than leave them at the end of her yard.

So, on my next – and final – visit I swept my arm across the rock, watching necklace, mirror, foil, keyrings, silver cutlery, and even a Welsh dragon souvenir bedecked in red glitter, tumble into the languid waves. They twinkled, briefly catching the sunlight as they sank, and then were swallowed by sand and murk.

My heart sank, too, as I returned to the dunes. I was running out of time.

I stripped down to my wetsuit, determined for one last underwater search. It was just after noon and the tide was on its way in, creeping halfway up the rocky promenade. After a whole morning under blazing summer sun, the waves felt almost tepid as I waded in to my waist. I pulled down my snorkel mask and bent my knees, ready to swim. The surf took me willingly.

A little way beyond the flat rock the first fronds of kelp extended from the ocean floor. I swam leisurely to this patch, and then over deeper water, closer to where I had first chanced upon the mermaid caught up in fishing nets.

I spent some time swimming face-down, breathing through my snorkel. Canvassing for unusual movement below. But the water was hazy, difficult to pick out much from this far away.

I took a deep breath and dived.

Seaweed slid past my fingertips as I parted clouds of swaying flora, entering an underwater forest full of beautiful, alien life. On any other day, this would be enough.

Too soon I shot up for air. Back down again, dodging a jellyfish and soaring carefully over the delicate corals.

Up, again.

Down, again.

It was a tiring cycle.

After an hour I swam to the end of the promenade and hoisted myself up onto the flat rock, basking in the sun. I removed my diving fins and let my feet splash in the water, enjoying the waves lapping up my legs with a faintly sucking sensation, like the sea would pull me off my perch and play with me again if I let it.

I released the strap on my mask and enjoyed the relief of sliding it off my head. The skin around my eyes was pink and slightly puckered from the seal, and I knew my mouth would be stuck in duck-face mode for another five minutes while I adjusted to breathing without a tube again.

The sunlight flashed across the mask. I held it up, admiring how it glinted in the golden sun. Well, why not? Something symbolic.

'This one's special,' I said to the undulating ocean. 'I hope you'll at least remember me by it.'

I wound up for a throw and pitched the mask as far as I could into the open water.

It landed with a satisfying *ploop* and instantly disappeared from view.

I turned to watch the waves breaking on the beach. A red kite circled lazily in the sky over the dunes. More birds hopped about on the ground. As I leaned forward, squinting to make out the shapes, I observed two gulls tugging at the straps of my black canvas bag. One of them got its beak inside and I saw a speck of white that was probably my sandwich.

I scrambled upright. 'Son of a–'

Something smacked me in the back of the head.

The shock of it made me slip. I lost my footing on the rock. Somehow I managed to stick the landing on all fours, splayed like an ungainly starfish with my fingers hooked into crags. The sea splashed over my legs as though it was laughing at me.

I fumbled back into a safe sitting position and looked around for the thing that had hit me.

My own snorkel mask lay on the rock by my side.

I picked it up with confusion – then sudden realisation. My gaze snapped to the rolling ocean, scanning for dark eyes above the waves.

'Are you out there?' I waved the mask in the air. 'This is supposed to be a present. From me to you.' Biting my lip, I tossed the mask back into the water.

Almost instantly it flew back out. I ducked and the mask slapped wetly onto the rock behind me.

A shadow lurked beneath the spot it had launched from. I craned my neck to peer further over the water, pushed one foot just a little too far over the edge . . .

A particularly strong wave washed up and over the rock, sucking my ankle from its perch. I went down with a yelp. My arm scraped against sharp rock as I hit the water. Saltwater flooded my mouth and nostrils. For a whirling minute I was at the mercy of the current.

And then I was caught – held close against a smooth chest, pulling up towards the surface. My face broke above the waves and I gasped for air.

'Urgh,' I spluttered, blinking seawater out of my eyes. My vision gradually un-blurred, forming the dark shape in front of me into the unsmiling face of the mermaid.

I was struck speechless. It was such a beautiful face. Yet so alien. Smooth slate-blue skin provided a gorgeous canvas for high, sweeping cheekbones and wide, almond shaped eyes. Nothing like human eyes. I couldn't tell if their depths held black-coloured irises, or if the pupils themselves filled the sockets; either way, the effect was of staring into an intelligent abyss.

The mermaid's arms were looped around my waist, keeping me buoyed above the water. Kelp fronds tickled my ankles. I was vaguely aware of a swooshing motion down below: quite likely, I thought, the sensation of a large fish tail holding balance.

'Hello,' I croaked. 'Thank you. For catching me.'

The mermaid pursed her lips – not the pouty expression of a Hollywood mermaid, but the thoughtful stance of a wary animal. I stared into unblinking eyes. She was figuring me out. I wondered if she could understand me.

Before I could open my mouth to speak again, the mermaid began towing me through the water back towards the rocks.

'Wait,' I protested feebly. Her grip was strong. She dragged me to the flat rock and lifted my arm against it. *Grab on,* I gathered she was trying to say.

Her head swooped in close suddenly, pulling my elbow up for inspection.

'Oh, no . . .' I said, following her gaze. A long gash stretched half the length of my forearm, spilling blood into the ocean. I must have caught it on the rock on the way down.

I swallowed thickly. A shock of wooziness hit my head as I watched the red rivulets run down my skin. 'H-elp,' I tried to say, but by then I was already going, going . . . gone.

The Sea-Dweller

Death fainted in my arms. It was alarming.

As her body went limp, the added weight pulled me underwater before I'd drawn a full breath. It took a confusing moment to right myself and haul her unconscious bulk above the waves again.

I propped Death's head on my shoulder. Still breathing. I couldn't understand what had caused this. The cut on her arm was ugly, but not deep – it did not look like she'd have lost too much blood.

I should not have sent the wave at her. I only meant to scare her off. And to stop her throwing more rubbish into my home. Now I had created a problem for myself.

I wanted to dump Death's body back on land and be done with it. But I could only get her so far. The tide was still climbing up the shore, and she risked drowning if she didn't awaken before the breakers washed over the entire beach.

The rocks might be safe enough.

I struggled to lift her. The task was more difficult than it should be. A conscious body will take some of the slack, naturally adjusting itself to float as best it can. But an unconscious one was like carrying a dead stone. Her limbs slapped me in the face as I hoisted her across my shoulders. I threw Death onto the flattest rock, and she rolled straight off the other side. I glared at the empty space. And reluctantly swam round to catch Death again.

The sea felt my frustration. Waves sloshed through Death's hair as I awkwardly held her up once more. We bobbed in suddenly choppy surf. A large wave carried us up high, then crashed down towards the rock ... I ducked away, dragging Death briefly underwater before popping up some yards away.

Calm, I sang. *Be calm.*

The waters were too open, too wild here. I might dash my own brains out on the rocks if I didn't take care. What to do?

I could let Death go, I considered. Release her to the ocean. She would sink to the bottom, drown in her sleep. Fish would strip her flesh. Her bones would become home to worms and crustaceans. She would be useful.

But the bones might be dredged up in fishing nets, and then more Death would come. Invading my ocean. Looking for answers.

Just like this one.

I prodded her cheek. The skin squished into her face, strangely elastic.

Death knew I was here. If I released her . . . she would only come back.

I turned my face into the wind, staring at the cliffs.

If I took her now, she wouldn't see the way . . .

The Land-Dweller

I came to, wet and shivering.

At first I couldn't work out whether I was truly awake, or caught in a dark nightmare. My eyes were open but could only discern amorphous shadows. The ground beneath me was hard and lumpy.

I stretched out tentative fingertips. They trembled over slimy surfaces, dipped into shallow pools of water. I could hear waves breaking nearby, though the sound was muffled. A deeply fishy odour clogged my nostrils.

My heavy breathing echoed around me. I remembered the sickly stream of blood and felt the sting reawaken in my left arm. I grabbed at it, fumbled stupidly as I encountered more alien sensations. Something slippery was wrapped around my forearm. In a burst of panic I thought it was an eel. I bolted upright and shredded it off my skin.

The thing fell away. As it settled over my palms I realised numbly that it was just kelp.

The shadows began to form into coherent shapes. A sense of walls and roof – a cave of some sort. A small hole, set high up in the wall behind me, let in a slim shaft of daylight overhead. Seemingly far away, seagulls squawked.

As I grasped more of my surroundings, my stomach tightened. I couldn't see a tunnel leading out. I was sat on a sort of rock shelf, slick with algae, and just wide enough for me to lean against the wall with my legs stretched out. Beyond my toes, a dark pool of water rippled to the edges of the chamber.

Calm down, I told myself through hitching breaths. *So it's a sea cave. Maybe this is as high as the water gets.*

The wall behind me was damp. My hands brushed over clusters of limpets, easy to distinguish with their pointy ridged shells. They clung tightly to nooks in the wall at least as far as I could reach. Waiting for the sea to return.

I fought to control my breathing, as though I were already underwater. Stay calm. It was important to stay calm.

How am I going to get out of here?

How did I get in?

I craned my neck to examine the hole. It was probably only a foot wide, and a good ten feet up. I might be able to climb to it. But the chances of my voice carrying far enough to be heard from outside were low. The chances of anyone passing close enough to hear it were even lower.

I stared at the water.

I'm a good swimmer, I reasoned. *I could always turn back.*

The thought I was avoiding was that the mermaid must have brought me here. The kelp on my arm ... was that her attempt at a bandage?

The cut had stopped bleeding, thank god. I could handle dried blood. But the mere sight of it in motion, from a living, breathing ... I put a hand to my mouth, swallowing the gulp of bile at the back of my throat.

That's it, I'd seen the blood and fainted in the water. So she had ... saved me? Repaying a debt?

The hairs on my arms prickled. I was suddenly assaulted by the feeling of being watched. I glanced up–

'Nefoedd!' The Welsh oath spilled from my mouth as I fell back against the wall. How long had she been there?

Utterly silent, the mermaid watched me from the water. She was mostly submerged, just eyes and nose above the surface. Two black voids in the gloom.

Now she rose a little further, revealed a narrow mouth. 'Nefoedd,' she echoed. 'Ein Tad yn y nefoedd . . .'

Our Father in heaven . . .

My ears pricked with confusion and bewildered memories of sitting next to my mam in church. 'That's . . . the Lord's prayer, isn't it? So you *do* speak!'

The mermaid cocked her head. I waited for a reply, but got the sense she was in turn waiting for me.

'What's your name?' I tried again.

She didn't like that. The mouth turned down in a frown. I startled as the still waters of the pool broke into little waves lapping at my shelf.

The mermaid emitted a series of clicks from her throat, and then in a flash disappeared underwater.

'Wait! I–' My brain garbled any sensible thing I might have said. I felt, with a cold twist of nerves, that I'd need her help . . . or permission . . . to leave this place safely. I reverted to my home tongue, the comfort of lilting Welsh syllables that fit so snugly in my mouth. *'Please don't leave me here.'*

The rippling pool stilled. It was eerie, the way the waves just rolled back on themselves. In the middle, the mermaid slowly rose again.

'Yo-u know these w-ords?' she said, in slightly broken Welsh. Her voice was lyrical, well suited to it.

'I do!' I replied excitedly. *'I understand you!'*

It was so hard to read her expression, but the drop of her shoulders suggested relief.

'Good,' she said. *'I did no-t want to kill you.'*

The eager smile froze on my face. *'Wh-what?'*

'If I co-uld not make you underst-and, I feared I m-ust kill you.'

She didn't seem nearly as perturbed by this statement as I was. The mermaid spread her arms over the surface of the pool, swaying gently from side to side while she floated. The motion of her tail treading water, I guessed.

'I'm . . . I'm glad you don't have to,' I said. 'Can I . . . go home?'

Finally, the mermaid blinked. 'We sh-all see.'

I stuttered a nervous laugh. 'Just, um. Tell me what I need to do.'

'You m-ust be not danger-ous.'

'Oh.' A weight lifted from my lungs. She was just scared. She was scared of me. 'That's– that's easy! I don't want to hurt you! At all!' I opened my palms, as if I needed to show her I had no weapons. Her head tilted down, looking toward my dive knife. It was secured to a bungee strap around my thigh.

Her eyes met mine again, this time with silent accusation.

'Hang on,' I said slowly. 'It's not dangerous.' Moving my hands at a snail's pace, I unsheathed the knife and showed it to her. 'Do you remember this? I used it to cut you free. Before. With the nets.'

'Get rid of it.'

Uncertainty gripped me. It was the only tool I

had on me. Apart from my wetsuit, I was essentially naked. But I was also in a mermaid's cave. And the mermaid was speaking to me. And oh my heavens, what would I have done just for the chance to speak with my mermaid only hours ago?

Wordlessly, I dangled my knife over the edge of the water, and dropped it in.

The mermaid nodded, apparently satisfied.

'You see,' I said softly, *'I'm not dangerous.'*

'You hunt-ed me.'

'What? I never . . .' I trailed off, remembering the relentless hours I'd spent combing the waters of the cove. The obsessive watch I'd held from the dunes. I'd even likened my gifts to fishing lures, shiny things to attract my prey. I'd wanted to reel her in.

I exhaled, searching for a way to explain. *'I'm sorry. I really didn't mean to scare you. I wanted . . . I wanted to see what you were. To find out more about you . . .'*

'Selfish.'

That word cut through me. That was Mam's word.

'I'm not selfish,' I declared. 'I'm– I'm– interested! It's not selfish to want to know things.'

'I do no-t want to be known.'

'That's a lie,' I countered. 'Otherwise you wouldn't have brought me here. You want me to understand you, right? So I don't hurt you? Please, listen to me.' I realised I'd been raising my voice, and did my best to soften it. 'Please, help me understand.'

The water swirled as she swam in a brief circle. Thinking? She didn't seem to know what to do.

The adrenaline was beginning to wear off and cold seeped under my skin. I rubbed my arms to keep warm. I couldn't wait around for her to decide. I cleared my throat. 'My name's Erin. What's yours?'

The mermaid paused and clicked her tongue at me.

'Sorry,' I said. 'I wasn't trying to be rude.'

She clicked again, and drew closer. 'That is my n-ame.'

'You speak in clicks?' Despite the situation, I squealed internally. Like dolphins! I was right! 'How do you know Welsh? This language we're speaking.'

*'I h-ave heard it spo-ken. For many y-ears. Once
…'* she stalled, on the edge of revealing something
more.

'Would you like a human name?' I asked, getting
ahead of myself. *'Then I could call you–'*

'No.'

She said it so flatly, I must have offended her.
*'I, uh. Just meant that I could call you something. I don't
think I can do those … those clicks like you did.'*

The frown returned, highlighting how neutral
her expression had been before. *'I h-ave been called
the w-ord* morgen.'

The word tickled another childhood memory.
*'I think … I think my mam told me fairy tales about
morgens. When I was little. Wild stories about missing
sailors and crystal palaces under the sea. Do you have
any of those down here?'* I joked.

She drifted backwards. *'No sailors.'*

'Ha, that's–' my voice dried up. As the mermaid
reached the far wall of the cave, a peculiar sparkling light fell over her body. It had been there all
along, dancing upon the water in the background
while I focused on our conversation. It was like

the rainbow lights of a prism, dispersing crystalline rays of colour through the air.

In fact, that's exactly what it was.

I followed the source of light to the hole above me, from which a bright shaft of sunlight hit the back wall of the cave. A wall covered, adorned, *gilded* in bright, clear crystals.

The light struck one cluster and was reflected into many others. As the clouds outside fully unveiled the sun for a fleeting moment, the light seemed to travel around the entire chamber. The walls lit up in sequence, suddenly sparkling in kaleidoscopic beauty.

The mermaid wore the light like jewels in the water. She was breath-taking.

The clouds returned. Far too soon the spectacle was snatched away.

'*That was … This is … Wow,*' was all I could say. My fear of the mermaid slipped away. *Help,* I thought dreamily, *I have fallen into a fairy tale and cannot get up.*

'*May I call you Morgen?*' I whispered, still overcome with the magic of it.

'*If you m-ust,*' she replied.

I grinned, relaxing against the rock wall. *'I shouldn't believe this, you know. Even though you're right in front of me. You're the stuff of legends and fairy stories.'*

'We tell stories about you, too.' She cocked her head to one side. *'We call you Death.'*

'What?' A light laugh spilled from my lips. *'What do you mean, you call us Death?'*

Morgen's dark eyes held me tight. I found myself suddenly humourless.

'You are our end,' she said. The water rippled outward from her, creating small waves. *'The end of all ends. Whe-n the fish have fled all waters and the corals turn to bone, we know Death has visited. Whe-n nets strangle and oils choke. It is the m-ark of Death.'*

Her words jarred me. They didn't belong in a fairy tale.

The pool began to froth and swell.

'That's not my fault,' I said feebly. Water bubbled at the edge of my shelf. *'It's other people, you know? Not all of us. Um, it's– what's happening?!'*

Waves broke over the rock and soaked my lap, hitting my core with ice. I hastily jumped up, but the water rose fast. It reached my armpits and I frantically kicked off to start treading water.

Morgen glided up beside me, indifferent to the sudden change of tide. Her hand settled into the small of my back, subtly aiding my buoyancy as the water lifted us both high up to the ceiling.

Soon we were level with the hole and I grabbed onto the opening, tried to claw my arms through. It definitely wasn't wide enough for my shoulders.

Through my frantic scrabbling, it eventually registered that the water had stopped rising. Morgen regarded me calmly. I withdrew my arms from the hole and took some deep breaths. My heart was hammering.

Looking out properly, the hole made for a good window to survey the cove and unfolding ocean below. Opposite this vantage point was the rocky half of the cove. That meant we were somewhere on the cliffside, possibly at the farthest tip where the land curved round . . .

Morgen pointed far out to sea, where the tiny shape of a freight ship crawled its way along the horizon.

'Explain thi-s. You leave trails of foul water and

poison. I can taste it from m-any miles away. All the ocean tastes of it n-ow.'

I stared at the freighter. It probably carried all sorts of cargo. Food so exotic that we've stretched all boundaries to make it commonplace on the table. Fresh pineapples and green mangoes. Fashionable shoes and affordable clothes. The latest smartphones, all wrapped up in plastic and polystyrene.

That's not me. I'm not Death.

'Corporations,' I choked out. Morgen looked at me blankly. *'Big industry, you know? We're trying to . . . fix things. We're trying. I promise that's not me.'*

Morgen let go of my back, and it dawned on me just how deep the water must now be beneath me. It had been, what, ten feet from my ledge to this hole? And how many more to the entrance of the cave below that?

I waggled one arm through the hole. Dimly hoped that someone might see it. Morgen didn't seem to care that I may be visible, and simply continued staring at the freighter.

As I looked over my shoulder to check the water level, another rocky ledge caught my eye. A round protrusion, wreathed in more sprays of crystal. But more interesting was what lay nestled on top of it. Pale spheres, maybe half a dozen, arranged in a small heap. They seemed strangely translucent as a ray of sunlight briefly washed over them.

Gravity unexpectedly yanked on my arm. I found myself clinging desperately to the hole as the water receded. It was down to my waist already.

Morgen looked up at me impassively. *'You should let go.'*

The water level reached my knees. 'Oh god,' I moaned, and let go. Because I was near the roof it felt like falling from a great height, and my stomach flipped. In reality I only dropped a metre or so under the water. No worse than jumping into a swimming pool.

I surfaced with a gasp, and within thirty seconds my feet touched rock. I stood stock-still, a little shellshocked, as the water drained away over the lip of my ledge. It settled back into a calm, flat pool once more.

'H-how–?' I stuttered, quaking with chills. *'Is it going to do that again?'*

Morgen shook her head, a weirdly fluid motion

that looked more like an eel veering left and right. *'The ocean he-ars me. We sing to each other. Dance to-gether.'*

'Is that a riddle or ...' the smart comment died on my tongue. *'Do you mean you control the water? You control the water?'* I exclaimed it again in English, as if one language wasn't enough for the revelation.

'No control,' she replied. *'Sometimes I a-sk. Mostly we j-ust sing.'*

'Is that how you got me in here? There's an entrance down there, right?' I asked, pointing into the pool. *'I don't think you could swim me underwater while passed out. Unless you have some kind of magic for that, too! Ha!'*

I rubbed my face and then my fingers, once again feeling the cold, brought on by the absurdity of it all. Yes, let's have some nice hypothermia for a dose of reality.

'I think I understand,' I said, meeting Morgen's poker-faced gaze. *'You're afraid that if you let me go, I might tell other people? Bring ... bring death to your home?'*

Her head tipped forward in a brief nod.

'Then let me make you a promise,' I continued earnestly. *'I swear, on … on …'* What might she consider sacred? *'… on my own home, on my family, that I will never tell anyone about you. I won't even come near this bay again, if that's what you want. I'll leave you alone forever.'*

Gosh. Had I always been such a good liar?

There was nary a twitch from Morgen's face as she studied me. *'That is a so-lemn oath.'*

'Yes.'

I waited for her give some further acknowledgement. She stayed silent. There seemed to be a frustrating chasm between us, as if there was some additional language barrier I couldn't cross.

I noticed the water was calm, though. It struck me that maybe I was looking in the wrong place to read her emotions.

Tentatively, I leaned forward, placing my hands on the edge of the rock shelf.

'So. We're practically friends now,' I said, with a hopeful smile. *'Perhaps you can show me the way out? Now you know I'm not … dangerous?'*

Morgen's inky gaze held mine for an uncomfortable second.

'*We sh-all see,*' she said. With a gentle push she glided backwards and slipped underwater. There were a few surface ripples, and then absolute stillness. The water neither rose nor fell.

It took a moment to catch up to me. She'd just gone. And left me here. In this cold sea cave. With no food or water, and the light was fading outside.

'Oooooooh, jeeeeez,' I hissed through my teeth. *Don't panic. Don't panic.*

I had some basic survival training. What to do if you were washed out to sea, or stranded on rocks far from the shore. Mostly, the advice was to get somebody's attention. Stay calm and get your partner's attention. Because only an idiot would go out on their own.

But I had to be selfish about it. I probably could have persuaded Rhys to join me on my mad mission. But I'd practically pushed him away. I wanted the mermaid all to myself.

Had I even told anyone where I would be today? Rhys thought I was on the North coast! And Mam . . . she'd think I'd just run away again. Ditched the snorkel job for a new adventure.

Don't panic, don't panic, don't panic!

I had to find heat. Goosebumps pimpled every inch of my bare skin.

I got on my feet, did a few quick star jumps. That's it, keep the blood pumping. Morgen would be back soon, right?

She hadn't said *anything* when she left.

Did she know how long humans could survive without food or water?

What if she didn't come back all night?

What if she did – and had decided not to trust me?

I collapsed to my knees and stared into the dark.

The Sea-Dweller

I needed time to collect my thoughts. Mother would have urged me to let Death go. She was kind, like that.

I couldn't deny the truth of our first meeting. Death had freed me from the nets. Death had saved my life.

Was that enough?

I freewheeled in the surf, letting it carry me. A quick flick of my tail brought me inches from the surface. I rolled onto my back, allowed my mouth to graze beyond the water's seal and sucked in a full breath. Then I fell backwards, headfirst in a lazy somersault, back into the kelp forest where it was easiest to hide from prying eyes.

The scar on my stomach twinged. The iron spike had been difficult to remove, but it wasn't the first piece of Death's refuse to have marred my flesh.

I sought out the patch of coral where the wrasse congregated in hungry swarms. Carefully pacing my lungful of oxygen, I settled down over the rocky reef, awaiting their services. Initially spooked, the little fish soon returned in a colourful cloud of shining scales. They nipped across my skin, cleaning away dead tissue and tiny parasites.

It was a relaxing ritual. But always bittersweet. So many memories of holding Mother's hand while the cleanerfish did their work. So many songs we sang while we waited, untroubled in the steady to and fro of the ocean.

Our songs contained our names. Mine was the sound of water lapping on rocks. Music of land and sea. My mother's name was the pull of the tide under a cloudy sky. We sang of storms and moonlight, and of glowing kelp and dark shadows in the reef.

She'd travelled farther than I, and would sing of dancing with glittering schools of mackerel, of racing from the jaws of silver seals along the cliffs, and of duets with whales held in the deep sea.

Your songs are beautiful, I told her once. *I wish one day mine will be as fine as yours.*

You are the most beautiful song I have ever sung, she replied, stroking fingers through my hair. *One day you will sing your own clutch of young into the ocean. Treasure them.*

I looked up to the speckled sunlight playing about on the waves overhead. The sadness in my mother's words was painful. She had lost all her eggs to the trawl of Death's nets. All but one.

I curled my hand around empty water, wishing my mother was here with me now.

She taught me to live with Death. To accept its unshifting presence on the cusp of our world. Long ago, we would swim to a spot below a church built on the cliffs and listen, for hours. In the church, Death spoke lovely words which drifted to us on the wind, and sang even lovelier songs which lit up the evening sky. Such beautiful songs. *'Ein Tad yn y nefoedd ...'*

The last of the wrasse finished their cleaning and pulled away from my flesh. I trilled a thank you and pushed away.

The ocean was turning dim. I skimmed the surface once again for a silent breath and lay motionless on my back, just a few inches under the water, admiring the glow of the rising moon.

This Death only wanted to see me. She had no harpoons or nets or hooks. She'd dropped the evil little knife.

I had not sought Death out, this time. I did not go to her in anger. Maybe this time would be different.

Maybe this time, I could do better.

The Land-Dweller

Diving in was a mistake. I should have stayed on my ledge where it was relatively dry. I could have tried to dry out my wetsuit, accumulated some body heat to stave off the threat of hypothermia.

And then what? Settled down to sleep in this dank, cold, wet cave while I waited for the supernatural fish lady to grant me another audience?

My enchantment with the whole situation was *thoroughly* dissipated.

Now, for the third time, I attempted going back underwater. Before submerging completely, I clung to my ledge while I took some deep breaths. The cold constricted my lungs; I couldn't seem to adjust the way I normally would on a dive.

You wouldn't normally be freezing to death.

I sucked in as much oxygen as I could, and dipped under. I pulled myself along the walls, feeling into nooks of crystal to crawl my way down, down . . . *so* far down, and still no opening to suggest an exit.

I thought I'd covered nearly all of its surface area by now. Surely I was near the bottom.

I pushed harder. Just a little more.

Still my feet dangled in empty water. My toes stretched to feel for solid ground that wasn't there.

How was I going to get out if I couldn't even hold enough air to reach–

Panic punched the breath out of me. I shot to the surface and exploded back into blessed air with relief. I was shaking. Fatigue had me making stupid mistakes. I couldn't stay in the water any longer.

It was also terribly dark. I wasted five minutes feeling my way around for the rocky ledge, and another five struggling to haul myself onto it. I felt so weak.

'Please don't let me die here,' I mumbled.

My eyes fell closed for few minutes while I hugged myself against the wall. When I jerked awake with a snort, I'd lost all sense of the passage of time. Had I been asleep for five minutes, or five hours?

The moon was high enough that some of its light now trickled in through the hole. The crystals twinkled like stars all around me. Their light reflected off the water, giving unnatural luminescence to the chamber.

My eyes wandered from the pool to the ceiling. If not down, why not up?

Beyond the hole, a few real stars were visible in a cloudless sky. Maybe I could scrape the little window into a larger opening, somehow.

I clambered upright, gave my face a couple of slaps to wake me up properly.

'Okay, let's do this,' I hissed under my breath.

The cave walls were plenty bumpy, and the crystal outcrops provided abundant hand and footholds as I began my ascent. But it was still hard going on my weary frame. Even my muscles felt groggy. I began to sweat in my wetsuit, adding an extra layer of clamminess to my discomfort.

Halfway up, I realised I'd meandered too far left of my target by following a route of the easiest handholds. But this blunder had steered me closer to the other ledge – the one I'd spied up high, when the chamber was filled with water.

I should check it out, right?

With another ten minutes of scrambling, I made it all the way across and touched my toes down on the ledge. There was less space on this one than my shelf far below. I hugged the wall until I felt safe to slowly crouch, and continued exploring it on hands and knees. The rock here was drier, bare of algae or seaweed.

Well, almost bare. My fingers sank into a crackling mound of dried kelp. It was piled up with a circular depression in the middle, like a nest.

And inside lay what could only be eggs.

I counted seven. They were large and spherical. I guessed they were the size of ostrich eggs, but rounder, with a pearlescent lustre that gleamed in the moonlight.

'Weird,' I breathed. Morgen's twinned human and dolphin-like qualities had me thinking she was a mammal. I would have expected her to give live birth, if I'd thought about it at all until now.

Weren't there some mammals that could lay eggs? Was the platypus one of those?

Was this really what I should be concerned about, right now?

I tried to shake the fogginess from my head. My focus was wavering.

I touched one of the eggs. It was warm. A shadow shifted under the translucent shell and I yanked my hand away.

As I stared, a thrill ran down my spine.

Imagine if I took one?

No one even knows you exist, I thought. *Imagine how much they'd love you, if they did.*

Imagine how fast we'd clean up the oceans, if we knew there were actual people living in it. Even if ... even if things didn't change straight away. There'd be new laws, right? Mermaids would have to be classed as a new endangered species, at the very least! We could ... we could protect this cove! Make it a mermaid sanctuary!

My mind filled with feverish visions. Of me handing over the egg to a group of very impressed scientists. Of galvanising a whole community into action ... I pictured all of Glamorgan alive with protests and placards. *Save The Mermaids.* There would be news crews and celebrities and maybe even David Attenborough would come down to see the mermaid for himself, and I'd receive a Nobel Peace Prize and maybe they'd even name the cove after me. Then Mam would see I wasn't selfish, once and for all.

The egg wasn't heavy. It felt so delicate in my palms.

I peered over the ledge. It was difficult to make out the pool in the dark below. Perhaps if I jumped from this height, I would reach the bottom faster and find the exit before running out of air. Risky.

Movement caught my eye – ripples over the water. Morgen emerged, water pouring over the curve of her shoulders. She made straight for the rock shelf, paused, and looked around in alarm.

Oh, shit. I glanced at the nest. My skin tingled with sudden chills. *I bet she won't like me being up here.*

As I tried to lean out of sight, my foot nudged a loose pebble over the edge.

It landed with a deafening *splash.*

Morgen looked up. Her eyes met mine. Wide. Fearful. *Angry.*

The mermaid's jaw yawned open, releasing a shrieking scream. The pool foamed into action, bubbling like a jacuzzi as it surged upwards.

'*Wait!*' I shouted. '*Just wait! Let me explain!*'

The mermaid bared teeth, sharp needles hidden behind her lips. Like a wild animal. Like a monster, ready to tear me apart. The water slapped at the walls in waves as it carried her higher and higher.

I scrabbled desperately away from the edge, back pressed against the unforgiving rock. I told myself she was just scared, she was just scared–

She was going to kill me.

'*Stop!*' I held the egg aloft over my head. '*Stop or I'll break it!*'

I don't mean that, I thought hysterically. *I wouldn't actually do it.*

The water kept rising.

'*I mean it!*'

The water was nearly at the ledge. The mermaid lunged upward–

Backed into the wall, I grasped the egg in both hands and *squeezed.*

A nauseating little *pop* cut through the mermaid's scream. Suddenly she was silent. The water turned utterly still.

Numb with shock, I dimly registered warm fluid running through my fingers. Dripping onto my toes.

'*L-let me go,*' I said. The deflating egg pulsed in my hands. '*Or I'll–* . . . *I'll hurt it more.*'

The mermaid's skin paled to a sickly grey. Her lips slowly closed, tightening into a thin, tense line. With no other visible emotion, she backed off.

'*What do you w-ant?*' she asked in a voice barely above a whisper.

Tears spilled down my cheeks. '*Please just let me out of here. Let me go home. I don't want to hurt you.*'

The water gurgled to life again and for a fearful moment I thought my time was up. Then the pool belched. An object erupted from its middle: planks of wood, a solid platform floating on the water. With a start, I recognised it as part of the little wooden jetty from the cove's beach.

A wave pushed it towards me.

'*P-ut it down,*' Morgen said. Her eyes were fixed on the egg.

'I'm sorry,' I said faintly. *'But I'm holding onto this until I'm safe.'*

Tiny ripples betrayed the mermaid's trembling.

Yes. I would tremble in front of Death, too.

I stepped onto the makeshift raft and sank to a stable sitting position. I cradled the shrunken shell. Its surface was crumpled, collapsing in on itself, and my hands were covered in a clear, viscous fluid. I felt so very cold inside.

I became aware of the walls moving. Or rather, of the water level descending. Morgen kept her distance. Watching.

The lower rock shelf passed my eyeline. Below this height the walls were green with life, encrusted with barnacles and the odd starfish. It was a long way down. A whooshing sound indicated the rush of water through an opening, and suddenly I was bouncing in rapids. I squealed, clutching the egg in one hand and the side of the raft in the other as I was carried through a tremendous archway, the water still dropping and frothing as it clashed with the sides of the rock tunnel, and then I was hit by fresh air and glorious, open space as my raft hurtled out into the sea.

Behind me, I glimpsed the top of the cave

opening. It was already being covered by rising waves. I thought I knew every inch of this shore-line. The cave must be ordinarily hidden, sealed by the ocean unless the mermaid ordered it not to be.

No one would have ever found me.

The wind ruffled my hair. Pale streaks of pink were a welcome colour in the sky. Early dawn twilight.

I realised I couldn't see Morgen.

Was there a dark shape under the water, or was I imagining it?

The pebble beach was a good fifty metres away. I could swim it easily . . .

Hugging the egg sac – for now it was definitely more sac than shell – to my chest, I tried to use one arm to paddle the raft towards the shore. It was useless. From the corner of my eye I saw a grey dorsal fin streak through the water. My hand involuntarily squeezed around the tiny embryo. I felt it quivering in my fist.

'Take me to the beach!' I shrieked to the ocean. I held out the formless lump, bulging through my squeezing fingers. Another flash of dorsal fin drove me to hysterics. *'Do it! Do it! Do it!'*

The quivering ceased.

My fingers opened and the thing slipped from my hand. It broke through the waves with a quiet plop.

An ugly sob built in my throat.

I cried mutely, shoulders shaking, snot dribbling from my nose. I never meant for . . . I never intended . . . I wouldn't ever . . .

'I'm so sorry,' I whimpered.

A new sound reached my ears. A high-pitched keening, nearly musical, on the edge of being a wail. I saw the mermaid then. Her back arched out of the waves, head thrown skyward and mouth gaping wide.

A solitary wave lifted her higher, pushing more body, more tail and fin out of the water until she was practically surfing on her tremendous fluke. It was the same shape I'd identified on our first meeting, but I had the proportions all wrong, obscured by shadows and murk. Her tail end was easily three times as long as the torso, and now revealed clearly in daylight and open air, I saw the underside of her tail was a bright white.

Suddenly I thought of orcas. Killer whales. Intelligent predators.

The monster dove towards me. I covered my

face with my arms. The raft tipped up, forced me to swipe for purchase, and then saltwater crashed down over my head and I was swirling, rolling, in a boiling current.

My head broke briefly through the waves and I drew in a breath. Then I was pushed down again, back into the dark. Something hard smacked into my ribcage and I reflexively grabbed on – the raft!

I clung tight as it buoyed to the surface. But as soon as I reached air, another wave was waiting. For a split-second I heard the mermaid's awful keening, glimpsed black clouds overhead, and then the pressure of water all around me, forcing me down . . . down . . . down . . .

The Sea-Dweller

I was lost in fury. Grief had its hooks in me, but fury was so much louder, so much more familiar. I sang my fury into the sea, and it listened.

Death was held below. The ocean wormed into her ears, her nostrils, fought to prise her lips wide open.

I sang of slaughter and storms. Of betrayal and retribution. Of innocence lost. And justice. There would be justice.

This was how it had been back then. When the fishing trawler had crushed my siblings in their helpless egg sacs. I felt anger. I felt *rage*. I sang it into the ocean and filled it with storms. This is my new name, I sang. Call me the rage of the sea. Call me the screams of those you have destroyed. Call me a song of vengeance.

I sank that boat. But men survived. They returned. With harpoons and other metal things that could hook and bite and maim.

Mother wouldn't flee while I faced them with my song. She should have . . . she should have . . .

I would make Death pay.

I called the ocean to release its hold on her. Death emerged, blubbing water from every orifice. The pitiful raft was smashed to pieces. She clung clumsily to a fragment of driftwood.

'*You murder me,*' I screamed through howling winds. '*You poi-son my waters and strangle my children. Y-our evils will be punished!*

She didn't seem to be listening.

'*Mam!*' she sobbed to the skies. '*I don't want to die, Mam, I'm sorry, Mam . . .*'

'*You are s-orry!*' I shrieked, sending another lash of waves over her head. I let it fill her lungs before allowing her plank to breach the surface again. She vomited water, gushing from her mouth and nose.

'*M-mam,*' she burbled like a child. Her head bobbed just barely above the waves.

She was pitiful. As spineless as a jellyfish. Thoughtless as a flatworm.

Somebody's child.

Clinging for dear life, begging for her mother.

Death's child.

Tears streamed from her eyes while her mouth wailed.

Your mother would have sung you songs, I thought painfully. *Such beautiful songs.*

Death lost hold of her driftwood and sank in the roiling foam. I dipped below the waves and watched as she tumbled head over heels in the ruthless current. Her arms flailed madly, grasping for purchase that didn't exist. Finally she couldn't hold onto her air any longer and a cloud of bubbles exploded from her mouth.

She sank, clutching at her throat, fighting against the water that was so eager to enter every airway. Her legs kicked madly, to no avail. I swam above, staring down at her struggling form.

Her eyes met mine. Bulging wide, bloodshot.

Screaming, silently.

I felt hard, like crystal. Sharp edges and hard lines. Waves that could cut through ships, smash cliffs into rubble.

Crystals look beautiful but cannot sing. Who

will sing for your children if you are made of crystal?

I let myself tumble in the current. Death was tumbling, too.

My mother was never angry. For all Death did, she was never angry. *Weakness,* I said. *We should drown Death. Chase it from our waters.*

Death has no malice, she told me. *Death is ignorant. Death is clumsy. Leave the creatures alone.*

She tried to save the men I drowned.

Death has children, too, she said, cupping the face of a young one. She took their bloated bodies to the shore, where the families might find them. She knew they might find us, too, but she did it anyway.

In front of me, my Death went limp in the water. One less Death in the world.

She had called for her mother. Hadn't I called for mine?

Fury seeped out of me, like blood from a wound. All that was left was grief. One less egg, one less young, one less beloved. One less, one less, one less.

Death is now one less.

I closed my eyes and sang my grief into the sea. The heaving waves dispelled, hushed into sorrow. Cool waters accepted my tears. The current swept Death into an embrace, lifting her into the tide. Together we carried her to the shore.

Scraping my flesh on unfamiliar stones, I pulled the water from Death's lungs. Gave her my own breath. Waited until her eyelids flickered, then hastily returned to the sea.

I watched from the cover of the rocks. She sat up unsteadily. Woozy from low oxygen. Her head wobbled as she scanned the horizon. My storm had broken, and light rain droplets now pattered onto a calm ocean.

Death turned and crawled for the dunes.

Stay away, I thought. *Find a reason to sing lovely songs. Elsewhere.*

I watched her until the sun climbed high in the sky. She rummaged among black bags and cried incomprehensible syllables into a shining device in her hand. Soon a vehicle with flashing lights and a crew in green uniform arrived. They covered her in silver foil and shone lights in her eyes before taking her away with them.

For a moment I wavered. As they bundled her onto a makeshift bed, I could have summoned a great wave. As tall as any church. It would have swallowed the beach and the dunes, and all the Death atop them. But I did not.

I sank back into my cool waters, and I let Death go.

Death

'Are you serious?' Rhys studied me with concern. 'You want to hand in your notice?'

'Yes,' I said.

'Why?'

'It doesn't matter.'

'But you *love* this job!'

I placed the rest of my paperwork on his desk. I couldn't meet his eyes. 'I can't go back in the water, Rhys. I just . . . can't.'

His weathered faced softened. 'Oh, Erin. Look, we've all had . . . experiences. You know, bad circumstances, slips in judgement. Did I tell you about the time I got my foot caught under a rock? Thought I was gonna drown for sure–'

'I know,' I interrupted, a bit harshly. 'I know you're trying to help, Rhys. Thank you. But it's not that I'm afraid to go back. It's just that I . . . shouldn't.'

'Do you need a raise? I could– '

'No. Thank you.' I paused by the door. 'Really, thank you. Goodbye, Rhys.'

He slumped. 'Bye, Erin. Take care of yourself.'

Ha. Take care of myself. Had I ever done anything else?

I walked along the cliffs, inhaling deep breaths of cold coastal air like a drug. I was giddy. Giddy to be alive.

Was it luck? Or had Morgen allowed me . . . allowed me to live? After what I did?

I scanned the sparkling ocean. Soon these waters would be alive with tourists, with pink flamingo inflatables and polystyrene surfboards and plastic ice cream wrappers fluttering on the breeze. And beneath them all I imagined Morgen, clasping her clutch of eggs and hiding, hiding from all of the loud, witless creatures above. I didn't deserve to trespass in her waters any more.

I reached a picnic bench and sat down. My phone was heavy in my hand. I'd been hovering over my mother's number for the entire walk.

'Suck it up,' I said to myself.

I pressed to dial.

Three rings. She wouldn't want to speak to me.

Two more rings. She probably won't–

She picked up.

My heart burst as I heard her voice. She was tentative. Was everything all right, she asked? It had been so long since I'd reached out to her.

'I'm okay,' I told her honestly. 'I'm working on myself. How are you?'

She opened up. Gave me words that felt like home. She showered me with inane questions – my health, my happiness, my job – and it was nearly an hour of warm, contented chatter before I got round to a question of my own.

'Mam? I was wondering. Does your friend still have that job opening?' I smiled at her enthusiastic response. 'Yeah. In the marine conservation department. Yes. I think I'd like to . . . I want to help.'

A weight lifted from my shoulders. Not guilt, not all of it. Maybe apathy. That comfortable, numbing shroud that would rather find a fairy tale than the ugly truth. I shrugged it off, and watched it swirl away on the fine ocean breeze.

About the Author

Georgina Jeffery is a British author of speculative fiction. Her stories often blend elements of fantasy, humour, and horror, and tend to reflect her fascination with folklore from around the world. You'll find mythical beasties, malevolent spirits, and eldritch magic in a lot of her writing.

Georgina's work can be found in a variety of anthologies and journals, including *The NoSleep Podcast*, *Unbreakable Ink*, *The San Cicaro Experience*, and *Copperfield Review Quarterly*.

ALSO BY GEORGINA JEFFERY

The Jack Hansard Series: Season One

Funny urban fantasy with a lot of British folklore. Jack Hansard, occult salesman, turns reluctant detective when his merchandise is stolen and becomes embroiled in a supernatural kidnapping case.

The Jack Hansard Series: Season Two

Jack Hansard and his coblyn friend Ang are back in business. Together they face shapeshifters, piskies, and ancient magics in their quest to track down Ang's missing kin and uncover the secrets of Baines & Grayle.

Beyond Thundering Waters (Dark Folklore)

A dark fairy tale in a modern Norwegian setting. When a young girl meets a huldra in the Norwegian wilderness, she unwittingly makes a supernatural bargain that puts her Pappa's life at stake.

Within Trembling Caverns (Dark Folklore)

A dark fairy tale in a modern Polish setting. A grandmother cares for an ailing dragon . . . but her compassion places her own family in the jaws of danger.

The Hub

A supernatural short story with a sci-fi edge. When an app developer accidentally creates a maliciously benevolent social media network, only her girlfriend can save her from what she's brought to life